Happy Birthday!

This notebook belongs to: ....

Made in the USA
Coppell, TX
18 February 2020

15972289R00069